THE FOREST FAMILY

THE FOREST FAMILY

Joan Bodger

Illustrated by Mark Lang

Tundra Books

Published in Canada by Tundra Books, *McClelland & Stewart Young Readers*, 481 University Avenue, Toronto, Ontario M5G 2E9

Published in the United States by Tundra Books of Northern New York, P.O. Box 1030, Plattsburgh, New York 12901

Library of Congress Catalog Number: 99-70968

Canadian Cataloguing in Publication Data

Bodger, Joan
    The forest family

ISBN 0-88776-485-1

I. Lang, Mark.   II. Title.

PS8553.O44F67 1999   jC813'.54   C99-930627-8
PZ7.B62FO 1999

We acknowledge the support of the Canada Council for the Arts and the Ontario Arts Council for our publishing program.

We acknowledge the financial support of the Government of Canada through the Book Publishing Industry Development Program for our publishing activities. Canadä

Printed and bound in Canada

1 2 3 4 5 6   04 03 02 01 00 99

For my dear niece, Mary Juhl-Diaz
J.B.

For Robin, Alexandra, and Caroline
M.L.

CONTENTS

PROLOGUE

A thieving magpie brought me a clawful of
jewels to arrange and rearrange in endless
patterns, until they made this story.

CHAPTER I

GREAT PAN IS DEAD

DAISY WAS JUST learning how to read, Rosy could count to a hundred, when their father went off to war. But they remembered him. The smell, mostly. Wood smoke and sweat, soap and something else. Ferns. Leaves. Fresh cut wood.

Their father's name was Bernardo, which means "bear" their mother said. Her name was Sylvania, which means "a place of trees." Sylvania was tall, slender, strong. Her hair was dark. Not black, but brown with purplish tints, a beech tree leaf in spring, before it turns to green.

Bernardo was as big as a bear, his daughters thought. He gave them big bear hugs and lifted each of them high into the air. They took turns riding on his back, holding on to his hair. His hair was thick and grew over his shoulders like reins.

"The color of honey," Daisy would say.

"The color of firelight," Rosy would say. But that was later.

Daisy was as fair as her father and Rosy, dark as her mother. Each was beautiful in her own way. They knew their parents loved them equally. They knew their parents loved each other.

"My girls," Bernardo used to say to them. "My three girls," including Sylvania with his daughters. He gave Sylvania big bear hugs too, coming up behind her after he had washed, while she was stirring the cauldron, or setting out bowls on the table. He would put his arms around her and put his face into the nape of her neck. Sometimes she would laugh and lean back against him; sometimes she would be cross and shrug him off.

"Not now," she would say. "Can't you see I'm trying to put food on the table?"

The Forest Family lived in a hut in the king's Forest. A stream ran nearby. There was a well and a garden and a small barnyard. Bernardo was a woodcutter; more than that, a forester. He knew not only how to cut trees down, but he was wise in the ways of the Forest. For every tree cut there must be three more planted, of the same kind. "One for the squirrels, one to rot, one to grow," Bernardo told his girls.

Although they lived far from any other families, the girls were not lonely because their parents peopled their lives by telling stories. They not only told "when you were a baby" stories, or stories about their own families and neighbors when they were young, but tales of kings and queens, of youngest sons and love-struck maidens, of elves and gnomes and forest fairies. Almost every evening their mother read to them from the thick leather-bound book her grandfather had willed to her.

One summer day, after a big storm, their father took them to a place where lightning had struck a tree and flames had blackened the hillside. He showed them the new seedlings that were already beginning to thrive in the ashes.

Bernardo told his daughters how each tree is guarded by its own special tree fairy. He told them about the elves and gnomes who mine for gold and jewels deep in the rocks, well below the dangling roots of the giant trees. As he spoke, a flock of birds flew down and hopped about at their feet. The birds picked up seeds from the new grasses that had pushed through, all the while keeping a bright eye cocked for worms. Bernardo explained how the birds distribute new seeds and how worms and beetles clean and tunnel the forest floor, weaving it back together again.

"My father and uncles taught me that the Forest knows what she needs and wants and *when* she wants it," he said. "They used to say that a good forester knows when to leave her be. She's her own sovereign."

"What does that mean?" asked Daisy.

"It used to mean that she was queen of her own destiny," said Bernardo. "Now she's dwindled down to be not much more than a fairy." He sighed.

"Tell us about the tree fairies," said Rosy, leaning against her father.

"Every tree has its own fairy," responded Bernardo. "It's the spirit of the tree; it lives in its wooden heart. Do you remember last Christmas when we burned the Yule log?"

"We saw the spirit then," said Daisy.

"Dancing along the log," said Rosy.

"Dressed in shining jewels," sighed Daisy, remembering.

"Rubies rich and red," said Rosy. (Rosy thought she *owned* the color red!)

"And topaz," said Bernardo, "like the center of a daisy."

His elder daughter flashed a grateful smile toward him. "And emeralds, like when we are in the deepest part of the Forest and light is sifting through the trees," she said.

"Speaking of which, just look at those shadows!"

exclaimed Bernardo. "Time to go home." They walked home in happy silence. Darkness and light dappled their path.

❦

"You don't have to go to bed so early tonight, girls," said Sylvania. "We'll wait until your sleeping loft cools off." After supper, Sylvania sat on a wooden stool outside the door of the hut, spinning thread on her wheel. The girls sat on the doorstep near her. Bernardo brought out his workbench from the shed. First he sharpened his axe, then he laid out his climbing tackle. He tested his ropes and straps, and checked the steel buckles as though his very life depended on them, which it did. Afterward he sat down on the doorstep with his girls, to mend a broken saw.

"A wondrous strange thing happened today," Bernardo said. "While Huw and I were deep in the Forest, sawing through an old oak, the saw rasped and refused to go any further. We seized our axes to hack into the trunk. You'll never guess what we found." With a flourish, Bernardo brought out a strange object and laid it on the table in front of them. "Do you know what this is?"

Sylvania and the little girls shook their heads, mystified.

"A stone axe head, very ancient. It must have been left there when the tree was a mere sapling. More than a thousand years ago, a man's hand chipped and shaped this little axe. He chipped and shaped so skillfully that his flint edge was sharp as my good steel. One day, must have seemed like any other day, he swung his axe at a young tree and bit deep into the wood with it. Then, he stopped! It's been stuck there ever since. All day I've been thinking about him, about that man. Year after year, century after century, a slow growth of pith and bark covered this perfectly made axe and encased it in the tree. It would still be hanging there if Huw and I had not chanced upon it."

"Is it ours?" asked Rosy.

"Can we keep it?" asked Daisy.

"No," said Bernardo, "we found it in the king's Forest. He holds the sovereignty of this land, so it belongs to him."

"You said that the Forest is her own sovereign," said Daisy.

Her father laughed. "Not any more," he said. "My axe maker probably believed that the Forest was sovereign, and that a king was king only when he was married to the Forest. Now we know better."

"Even so," said Sylvania, "I like that old idea. A good king should cherish his land and his people as a good man loves his wife and children. Maybe your axe maker was wiser than we give him credit for."

"I can't get that woodsman out of my mind," Bernardo said. "He's almost like a friend. I wonder what happened to him, to make him leave such a good tool behind? I hope no harm came to him. But short life or old age, he's just as dead, and has been just as dead, for more than a thousand years." Bernardo gave a little shudder, then he laughed.

"Now I've told you my story, it's time for your mother to tell one of hers. Tell us my favorite," he said. "The one about your great great-aunt, the famous pie maker."

"Not again! Why do you like that story so much?"

"Because it's about a woman who keeps her promise, no matter what." But it took more pleading and coaxing before Sylvania gave in. . . .

"Yes, it's true. If I do say it myself, my great great-aunt Sibyl *was* a famous cook and baker. She went to all the big houses in the neighborhood, and she was willing to cook for common folk, too. She took her own pots and pans and mixing bowls with her in two baskets slung from a yoke she balanced on her shoulders. Folks called her Yoke Girl.

"One day a man came with a written message, asking Yoke Girl to go to a farm on the other side of Crinkle Bank to bake for a funeral feast. The message said a carriage would be sent next morning to take her there. She had never heard of that farm before, which the note said was called Pan Edge, nor had she heard of the family, which was called Cutcat. But the pay was good and she was willing to go, even on short notice. Next morning, however, the man appeared at her door without the carriage. He said that the master's son had broken the axle on his father's phaeton by driving too recklessly along the high mountain roads. They would have to walk cross-country to Pan Edge in order to get there on time.

"Yoke Girl was willing enough. Her legs were sturdy and she was used to walking. She packed up her baskets, not forgetting to include her phials and twists of secret herbs and spices, and settled the yoke across her shoulders. Soon she was following the messenger who ran, agile as a clambering cat, up the path that goes over Crinkle Bank and down into the glen on the other side. By the time they started up to Pan Edge, her pots and pans and bowls were clanging in her baskets, and she was that short of breath she could hardly call out to him to slow down.

"When she got to Pan Edge, she was taken directly to the kitchen of a great house and instructed to make and bake her specialty, which was game pie. Pheasants and larks and rabbits, onions and parsnips and carrots were all set out for her on a marble slab, as were the makings for good rich pastry, enough for a dozen pies. She asked for a pitcher of beer for flavoring, measured out her herbs, and soon was up to her elbows in flour.

"At the end of the day, she washed up and repacked her baskets. Then she went to stand in the backstairs hall, await-ing her pay. The farmer came up behind her, so silent he might have been on padded paws. The hall was dark and full of shadows; she never did get a proper look at him. When he introduced himself as Farmer Cutcat, she bobbed him a curtsy. He handed her a purse full of money and said, 'You are a good cook, Yoke Girl. My guests fair licked their whiskers over your game pies. I am glad enough to pay you a good fee, and I will gladly pay you more if you do one more task.'

" 'And what might that be?' she asked.

" 'When you go down into Crinkle Glen, you will come to a hole in the rock. Stop there and call into it: *Tom Cutcat*

sez Great Pan is dead. If you will promise to do that, loud and clear, I will pay you three gold pieces in advance.'

"Well, it seemed little enough to do for such a bold price, so my great great-aunt promised. Then he told her to hold out her hand. As he pressed three gold coins into it, he raked her outstretched palm from finger roots to wrist with what for all the world felt like a great cat's claw. Before she could cry out in pain and protest, he was gone.

"As you may be sure, our Yoke Girl quitted Pan Edge as fast as she could. She ran along the path, clinking and clanking, the yoke swinging on her shoulders. The full moon lighted the path well enough, but when time came to go down into Crinkle Glen, the overhanging trees and rocks gave only bitty patches of light. By the time she came to the hole in the rock, she was that afeared and that resentful she would have run right by without stopping, except for one thing –"

"What was that?" Daisy and Rosy asked, already knowing the answer.

"No woman in our family ever breaks a promise," Sylvania said. "So my great great-aunt Sibyl stopped and put her hands up against the cold rock. Then, as well as she could, with the yoke bumping and her sore hand hurting, she stuck her head into the hole and called out, loud and clear: 'TOM CUTCAT SEZ GREAT PAN IS DEAD!'

"Immediately there was such a keening and a sobbing, such a wailing and a caterwauling, that she put her hands over her ears. Came a swirl of leaves and midges all around her, and a flight of fairies flying out of the hole chased her all the way up to the top of Crinkle Bank. When she got there, she could see the whole countryside – hill and dale, moor and mountain – spread out in the moonlight. And a great screech came out of the wheeling sky: 'WHAT? GREAT PAN IS DEAD? THEN I AM KING OF THE CATS!'

"There and then my great great-aunt dropped her yoke and ran all the way home. Next day she went back for her pots and pans. But of that farm on the other side of Crinkle Bank, she never heard more, nor did anyone in the neighborhood ever admit to know of a place called Pan Edge, or of a family called Cutcat.

"For the rest of her life, Yoke Girl bore that claw mark across her palm. But from that day until the day she died, she was a woman blessed with good fortune, as have been all the women in our family, ever since."

"And the proof of that," Bernardo said, winking at the girls, "is that all the women in her family, including herself, have married well." Then he and Sylvania laughed, and maybe she gave him a kiss. Or maybe she didn't.

"I think it's time for the girls to go to bed," said Sylvania.

"For all three girls," said Bernardo.

When she was in her nightgown, Sylvania did not immediately slide between the sheets with her husband. Instead, she stood for a moment at the window, gazing out at the night sky. "That story is not just about a promise," she said, turning to Bernardo. "My grandfather – he was a preacher and something of a scholar – used to tell us that the story is about the wheel of time. He said that his Aunt Sibyl had been chosen as a messenger to announce a break in the wheel, a break in the ordering of the stars and planets."

"What in Thunder does *that* mean?"

"That change is coming."

"Come to bed," said Bernardo. "Your family thinks too much."

CHAPTER 2

MEMORIES AND PREDICTIONS

DAY AFTER DAY a terrible heat hung over the Forest, only now and then abated by violent storms. Even when there was no storm, thunder muttered in the distance. Came that time of year when daylight equals night. A new wind swept through the trees; the sound of branches rattling against the house was like artillery fire. The Forest Family woke to find that, although the sky was blue and clear, there was a chill in the air.

With the change in the weather came a change in the Forest that was nothing to do with the season. A horde of men came crashing and blundering into the king's domain. They were the king's own miners, looking for iron. They blasted deep pits in the rich earth floor, breaking down root systems that had been there since the Forest began.

"What will happen to the badgers and the elves?" asked Rosy, worried. "And to the worms?"

When the miners announced that they had found the kind of rocks they were looking for, the king ordered that a large part of the Forest be cut down. Thousands of trees were burned into charcoal. The charcoal was used to heat the rocks to a temperature so high that the iron ore melted. Thick fiery liquid ran out into puddles and was ladled into molds, molds that looked like loaf pans. The iron "loaves" were called pigs. The king and his ministers ordered that the iron be forged into guns and cannons.

Several times Bernardo found an excuse to work in that distant part of the Forest. He wanted to see for himself what was happening. The miners' machinery filled him with admiration. But Sylvania was distraught. "I can't stand the noise," she said. "The very house shakes."

"And the dishes rattle on the shelf," said Daisy. "Sometimes we can't hear the birds. I'm beginning to think they've stopped singing."

"What is going to happen to them – and to the deer?" asked Rosy.

"The king must have a plan," said Bernardo. "He loves the Forest and he loves his subjects. He won't let any harm come to us."

"Let's hope you're right," said Sylvania. She moved

closer to the kitchen fire, hugging herself. "I keep feeling shivery," she said.

❦

The king ordered that the oldest oaks in the Forest be cut and sawed into planks to build ships that would trade with other countries. Bernardo took Daisy and Rosy to see one of these trees after it had been felled. Like a wounded giantess the oak lay on her side, exposing her raw rings for all to see and stare at. "Every ring means a year of growth," Bernardo told them. "This tree must have been more than eight hundred years old." He helped his daughters count the first few decades, but after a while they gave up.

"Poor old tree," said Daisy. "She must be wondering why she had to be cut down."

"What happened to the tree's spirit?" asked Rosy. "Where was her special fairy when the tree needed her?" Her father had no answer.

❦

When spring came, warm winds melted the snows and opened the roads to travelers. They brought rumors of war. Over the mountains and over the seas, there was a land that the king claimed belonged to him. Although other families had been living there since time began, he wanted them driven out so he could cut down their forests and dig in their mines. The king proclaimed that all the able-bodied men in his kingdom must join the army and go to war. Bernardo must leave his wife and children. He must leave his beloved Forest and go far away to fight men he didn't know in a land he didn't care about.

"I don't want you to go," said Sylvania. "What will we do without you?"

"Hush," said her husband, placing his hand across her mouth, "don't let anyone hear you say that. You will bring shame on me."

"Where are you going?" asked Daisy.

"What will you do when you get there?" asked Rosy.

"What will you bring us?" they chorused.

"I'll see the big world and I'll bring each of you a present," said Bernardo.

"I never thought 'til now you were a fool," said Sylvania. "Admit it. Part of you wants to go."

"You know I have no choice," he said. He put his arms around her and gave her a great bear hug. "You're always pretty when you're angry," he said. "What do you want? But remember, I can't promise you the moon."

Sylvania tried to laugh, but tears ran down her cheeks.

"That's my good little girl," her husband said, wiping the tears away. Then he kissed her, kissed each of his daughters, and was gone.

In the beginning there were letters brought by a passing peddler, or a soldier on his way to somewhere else. The first few letters were cheerful, with funny bits in them about learning how to march and getting used to new boots and how dreadful the food was. Then there was a letter, "written in great haste," saying that Bernardo was about to embark on a ship and sail across the sea to a strange new land. The voyage would take a month and he had no idea how he could send a letter, or any money, after that.

"What will we do without the money?" asked Daisy.

Sylvania had no ready answer for she, too, was worried, but she wasn't Yoke Girl's great great-niece for nothing.

"What will we do for food?" asked Rosy.

"Where will we live?" asked Daisy.

"We're luckier than most," said Sylvania. "We have the hut."

"And we have the garden," said Daisy.

"And we have the goats and hens," Rosy chimed in.

"Most important of all, both your father's family and mine hold ancient gleaning rights in the Forest," said Sylvania. That night she burrowed into an old blanket chest and found, buried deep, the commonplace book her mother had given her before she died. The grandmothers in her family, who could not write, had dictated to her mother all they knew of the things that grew in the Forest, and how to use them for cooking and healing and running a household. The book held all the accumulated wisdom of the women of her family.

One more letter came from Bernardo. Three sentences only: He loved his three little girls more than anyone in the world. He wanted them never to change. He wanted to be able to treasure them in his heart just as they were now, and as he knew they always would be.

But change happens. Daisy and Rosy grew taller. They lost their baby teeth and learned to help their mother with her work. Daisy liked to cook and sew and help about the house. She dreamed over soap bubbles and polished the copper kettle 'til it shone like the sun. Rosy liked to chop wood and dig in the garden. She splashed water from the pump, coped with the goats, and gathered eggs from the hens.

One evening the Forest Family (or what was left of it) sat before the fire. Sylvania opened the leather-bound book that had belonged to her grandfather and spread it out on her lap. While her daughters leaned against her, she pointed with her finger and helped each of them to sound out words that were too long, or too hard. Daisy read, quite well, the story of Joseph being sold down into Egypt. Rosy, who needed more help, chose the story about Jonah in the belly of the whale. Both stories were about people being lonely and far from home, which led them to think about Bernardo.

"Let's play the 'I Remember' game," said Rosy.

"What sort of game is that?" asked Sylvania. The girls explained that the purpose of the game was to remember everything they could about their father.

"I remember riding on his back when he pretended he was a bear," said Daisy.

"I remember how he growled," said Rosy. And she growled, to prove it.

"I remember his hair was long and springy on the back of his head," said Daisy.

"His hands are very big," said Rosy. "And his nails are . . . were . . . thick and broken."

"The hair on his arms was like gold wire," said Daisy.

"His eyes are blue with amber flecks," said Sylvania. "His lips were red and full."

"He laughs a lot," said her daughters.

"Yes, he did," said Sylvania. And she sighed. After that they played the "I Remember" game almost every night.

❧

On the first balmy night in May, Sylvania brought her stool outdoors, to her accustomed place by the doorstep. She was spinning. Daisy had snipped a long length of yarn from the spindle and was winding a skein onto Rosy's outstretched hands. When Rosy protested that her arms were getting tired, they changed places.

"Let's play 'I Remember,' " said Daisy.

"I'm tired of that game," said Rosy.

"I'm tired of it, too," said Sylvania, unexpectedly. "Let's, this night, not talk about the past. Let's talk about the future. About what is going to happen when your father comes home."

"He'll be handsomer than ever," predicted Daisy. "His hair will shine like the sun, and he'll be wearing a splendid uniform with gold buttons on the jacket. He'll have gold around his wrists, at the cuffs, and a gold stripe down each side of his trousers. And gold medals on his chest."

"What do medals look like?" asked Rosy.

"Like gold coins," said Sylvania.

"He'll have a sword," Rosy said. "Jeweled about the hilt, and he'll carry it in a jeweled scabbard that will shine with all the colors of the sunset. He'll be even taller than he used to be, and his boots will be polished to a fare-thee-well. He'll be riding on a horse with a beautiful saddle, and he'll open his saddlebags and bring out the presents."

This new game was so exciting that all through the summer they could hardly wait until supper was over and the table scrubbed before they sat down to predict the presents.

"He'll bring me silken thread and a silver thimble," Daisy said, "and a length of claret-colored velvet." She almost always predicted the same thing. Rosy, on the other hand, changed her mind often. For a while she thought that Bernardo would bring her a collection of little boxes, carved from ivory and rare woods. Then she thought she wanted a silver watch, like the king's. Bernardo had never actually *seen* that watch, but he had told his little daughter what had been described to him. He and Rosy both longed to see not only its beauty, but its mechanical wonders – how the little cogs and wheels revolved. They wanted to listen to the ticking, to hear the voice of a tiny bell as it marked the hour. Precisely!

Such talk made Daisy anxious. "Rosy, take care. We don't want to make the king angry. I think he would be cross if he knew that someone, especially a little girl, owned a watch just like his."

Rosy cheerfully changed her mind again. "I know! Father will bring me a bearskin rug. We can spread it out by the hearth, and you and I will be able to lie on it when we listen to stories."

Sylvania rarely entered the game. Since she would not choose a gift for herself, they said they would choose one for her. They wrangled for days over what would be most suitable, and finally agreed that they would let Bernardo present his wife with a necklace of softly shimmering pearls. "Each one like a little moon," they told their mother.

Sylvania, listening, was at first amused. But as time went by, she would sometimes interject: "I just hope he brings *himself* home. I think I can even endure his being wounded as long as he's his very own *self*." When another year had gone by, she said, wonderingly, "Sometimes I can't remember who he used to be. Or who *I* used to be."

~

"Today's the day I promised to take you with me when I go a-gleaning," said Sylvania early one morning. "I hope you've kept *your* promises."

"I've done the dishes and swept the whole house," said Daisy.

"I've fed the goats and fetched the water," said Rosy.

"Then we're ready to go," said their mother. First she led them to a sunny bank where they picked sweet-smelling thyme. She showed them how to tie the stems with string and put the bunches into their baskets. When they walked across a logged-off area and came to a place where sand and clay showed through the ground cover, Sylvania showed her daughters how to recognize sorrel ("good for soup") and dandelion leaves ("good for cooking with hocks and potatoes"). They also found pale flowered burnet (the leaves tasted like cucumbers). "Remember: even where the land seems barren, you can always find something to eat," said Sylvania.

In June, when they headed for the woods, Daisy paused at woods' edge. She had recognized the leaves of wild strawberries. Each berry was smaller than the nail on her little finger. Rosy's face lit up with expectation. "Only half for ourselves," said Sylvania, smiling at such obvious greed. "For every one you pick, another must go into your basket to sell to our customers." She pointed out the purple leaves and white flowers of a knee-high plant, which grew nearby. "In August and September you'll find berries there, too. They'll look like black cherries, but don't eat them. Don't even touch! They are the fruit of the deadly nightshade."

While her daughters were down on their hands and knees, picking strawberries, Sylvania busied herself in a patch of tall flowers that grew nearby. "These are foxgloves," she said, thrusting out a long stalk. It was studded with rows of pink tubes, each arrayed with a spatter of spots. Daisy, glancing up, said, "They look more like thimbles than gloves."

"Or like fat freckled fingers," said Rosy.

"Good for you! Both of you! Another name for foxglove is digitalis, which sort of means 'finger.' What's important for you to remember, though, is that digitalis juice is good for a pain in the heart."

"Will it cure a *broken* heart?" asked Daisy.

"Could it make you not so sad?" Rosy's voice was hopeful.

"I only wish it could," said her mother, startled. Bernardo was so far away from her, in time and distance, that sometimes a whole day would pass without her feeling that her heart was being torn asunder. There was only a dull ache now. Yet her sadness must still be visible, else how could her children have perceived her pain?

In the heat of high summer, the gleaners went even further into the Forest. Before they plunged into the shadows, Sylvania paused, looking for a certain kind of leaf. "This is mugwort," she said. "Here! Take some and rub it on your skin. It will drive off midges." Then she pointed to a large furry leaf growing near the ground. "That's dock," she said, "the cure for nettle sting. Wherever there are nettles, you'll find dock; wherever you find dock, there will be nettles." Rosy looked anxious. She had had experience with nettles.

Even so, it was not long before Rosy brushed up against some star-shaped leaves covered with green fuzz. The fuzz looked soft as velvet, but was actually a network of tiny hooks. When caught under her skin, they spurted a fiery liquid that felt like a bee sting. "Ow! Ow!" Too late she knew what she had done. Daisy came rushing with a dock leaf. Remembering mugwort, she would have rubbed the offending spot if her mother had not stopped her in time.

"No! No! Never *rub* a nettle sting! Just lay the dock leaf on the place where it hurts; the coolness of the dock will draw out the fire." It took several dock leaves before Rosy stopped jumping up and down and screaming.

When Rosy had been solaced, they sat in welcome silence, letting the sounds of the Forest sweep over them. Few birds sang, but they heard an occasional rustle in the underbrush, the sighing of wind through trees, the music of a distant brook. When a twig cracked. Rosy was about to cry out again, but

Sylvania put a finger to her own lips and pointed. "Look!" she whispered. They blinked in the gloom, at first seeing nothing. Then they made out a herd of deer. Does and dappled fawns drifted like spirits through the light among the trees.

CHAPTER 3

THE GLEANERS' TALE

TOWARD THE END of the summer, Sylvania took her daughters so far into the wilderness that the three of them spent the night there. When darkness came, they stopped for supper by a spring. Sylvania pulled some watercress from the bank and washed mud from the roots before she gave it to her daughters to munch. It was curly and crisp and very green. "Good for the blood," said Sylvania. She had brought bread and cheese with her, and they had picked blackberries on the way through the woods. While Sylvania built a little fire, Daisy and Rosy lay down on the thick layers of leaves and loam that cushioned the forest floor. For a while they were silent, gazing up through lofty branches to the stars.

"My bed is soft and springy as a bearskin rug," said Rosy, bouncing up and down.

"I must be lying on the best-smelling mattress in the whole world," said Daisy. She rolled over and buried her nose in rotting leaves and loam. After a while she sat up and brushed off the leafy bits from her face. "Tell us a story," she said. Rosy joined in with her pleading.

Their mother was sitting with her back against a tree so she would not sleep too soundly and could bank the embers all night long. "Yes, I'll tell you both a story if you like," said Sylvania. "It will help me keep awake."

"Tell us a love story," said Daisy.

"Tell us a story about gleaners," said Rosy.

"The great-aunts used to tell me about a woman they knew, or maybe just knew *about*. They said her name was Naomi Eliot. Or something like that. She and her husband, Mr. Eliot, lived in a place called Breadhouse, or maybe it was Brighouse, over in Yorkshire. They had two sons."

"What were the sons' names?" asked Daisy.

"Malcolm and Hilion," said Sylvania.

"How old were they?" asked Rosy.

"When the story begins? About ten and twelve," said Sylvania. "Times were hard in those days. Almost all of the Eliots' crop went to pay the taxes, and Mr. Eliot couldn't find work anywhere, so they leased their last couple of fields to a sort of second cousin and moved away."

"Where did they go?" asked Rosy.

"They went to a place called Moab, on the other side of the sea. I think it must be in France. Folk there spoke a different language and had a different religion. The Eliots lived in Moab almost ten years, but they didn't fare much better there than they had in Brighouse. It wasn't long before Mr. Eliot died, poor man. The strain had been too much for his heart. The only good thing that happened was that the sons married two women from Moab who were happy with their husbands and got along well with Naomi."

"What were the girls' names?" asked Daisy and Rosy, almost together.

"Malcolm married a woman named Oprah, and Hilion married a woman named Ruth. They were both poor and were both older than their husbands. Naomi could afford only the smallest bride price."

"Did they have babies?" Daisy asked.

"No. Before either of the wives conceived, their husbands were killed in an accident. The great-aunts told me that someone told them that *she* had heard that the two brothers had been running alongside a farm cart, loading stones, when the cart turned over and crushed them. The worst part of the tragedy for Naomi was that she had no grandchildren. She longed for a grandson to honor her husband and to carry on his name."

"This sure is a sad story," said Rosy.

"I don't know if I want to hear any more," said Daisy, putting her hands over her ears.

"Let me point out that you were the ones who asked me for a story," Sylvania said. "Things get better later on, but you have to help me make them happen. The people inside the story are relying on you to listen, or else they cannot *be*."

"I asked for a love story," sniffed Daisy.

"I wanted a story about gleaners," Rosy pleaded.

Sylvania sighed. "Trust me," she said.

"So Naomi was left all alone in a strange land. She had come to Moab with three men – her husband and their two sons. Now she was a widow, the head of a household of three widows – herself and her two Moabite daughters-in-law. She decided to go back home to Brighouse, in Yorkshire, where she came from. She told the two girls that they had better go back to their parents.

"Oprah and Ruth both came from large families with too many daughters. They didn't want to go home. They knew that their parents would treat them as a burden and make them work like slaves. Worse, their sisters and brothers and their brothers' wives would show them contempt. Or pity. *Pity from your own kind can be worse than contempt.* Oprah and Ruth had come from poor families and had married poor men, but Naomi had loved and valued her two sons as though they were wealthy and successful. She treated their wives as though they were special and precious. Oprah and Ruth found they had married into a rich family, rich with stories and songs and laughter. Rich in love and respect. They had never known such a household existed!"

"But *we* know it does," whispered Daisy.

"They should come see *our* house," said Rosy, snuggling down to listen.

"So the three women packed the few belongings they could carry and set out for the coast. They had gone only a few miles before Oprah lost heart. She said she was afraid to leave Moab to go to a country where no one spoke her language, and where the women practiced different customs. Her parents' home was beginning to look better to her with every step away from it, even though she knew that her family would treat her badly. Better the trouble she knew than the trouble she didn't know!

"Naomi was hardly surprised by the girl's change of heart. She kissed Oprah tenderly and gave her a warm and loving hug, along with her blessing. As she watched her disappear around a bend in the road, Naomi knew that she was gazing on Malcolm's wife for the last time. Not only was she losing Oprah, it was like losing her son again. It was like losing her husband again! With tears running down her cheeks, she turned her attention to Ruth, expecting her other daughter-in-law to leave her.

"'Go home, child,' she said. 'Go home to your mother where you belong.' But Ruth surprised her. She flung her arms around Naomi. She clung to her, weeping. 'Tell me not to leave you; tell me not to stop following you. Where you go, I will go. Where you live, I will live. Your people shall be my people, your ways my ways. When I die, let me be buried near you.'

"The two women took passage on a fishing boat and crossed the sea. They walked all the weary way back to Naomi's old village in Yorkshire. When news spread that she had come home, the women of Brighouse poured into the street, buzzing like bees. *Oh, how hard it is to take pity from one's own kind!* 'My name is no longer Naomi,' she cried. 'My name is Bitterness. I went out from this place full and I have returned home empty. When I left this place I had a husband; I had two sons. Now they are all dead.' Oh, she was bitter!"

"But she had Ruth," said Daisy.

"Yes, she had Ruth. And Ruth went to work for a rich farmer, a Mr. Boaz. *Squire* Boaz. Although she did not know it at the time, he was a nephew of her father-in-law, Mr. Eliot."

"What did she do?" asked Daisy.

"She was a gleaner."

Rosy had been half-asleep. Now she sat up. "Like us?" she asked, excitedly.

"Not exactly. We are forest gleaners and we work for ourselves. Ruth worked for Mr. Boaz. After the crop is cut with a scythe and gathered into sheaves, there are always stalks and heads of barley, even separate corns, to be picked up from the ground. Farmers hate to see the smallest grain go to waste! The gleaners must stoop and crawl, stoop and crawl, inching along the ground. They work in hot sun and dust, cold rain and mud. Their eyes ache and their heads whirl with the effort of distinguishing good grain from straw, kernel from pebble. Their knees hurt and their backs hurt; their hands bleed from being cut by the stubble, cruel as broken glass. The work was too hard for Naomi. Ruth did the work for both of them, to earn whatever money she could.

"Mr. Boaz noticed how every day Ruth gave her money and part of the dinner he provided to an old woman who came to meet her. Ruth was so loving that he took for granted that the older woman was her mother. He was amazed to find that Naomi was Ruth's mother-in-law. Several times he stopped to chat with the two women. One day, when Naomi

and the squire were talking, they discovered the connection, that Mr. Eliot was his uncle. He was astounded to hear their story: how Naomi had journeyed to Moab and back, and how Ruth had chosen to journey with her to Yorkshire. He found he couldn't keep his eyes away from the young woman who had come so far, from a land across the sea. He regarded her with great respect. This was a woman of strength and courage! More important than that, he perceived how kind she was.

"Mr. Boaz fell into the habit of gathering leftovers from the workers' tables every day. He did it himself, so his servants wouldn't take notice. He told Ruth to hide the bowl under her shawl and to take the food home to her mother-in-law. He instructed his men to guard the well when the gleaners went to fetch water on their way home. He knew that there were young laggards who hung about the well. They whistled and pushed, touched where they shouldn't touch, calling names and laughing at nothing at all. The other gleaners all understood that it was on Ruth's behalf that Squire Boaz had posted a guard. Sometimes they teased her. Or insulted her.

" 'Why are you doing this? Why are you being so kind to me?' Ruth asked him.

" 'Because *you* are so full of loving kindness to your mother-in-law,' was his reply.

"Do you remember those two fields that Mr. Eliot had rented out? He had leased them to another relative, a second cousin. By terms of the agreement, that cousin was allowed ownership of the land if Mr. Eliot, or any of his heirs, ever returned to Brighouse but did not work the land. Naomi was her husband's heir and Ruth would be Naomi's heir. Neither Ruth nor Naomi was able to plow and plant the land that used to belong to Mr. Eliot. (Oh, how Naomi raged that she had no son!)

"Now you two girls listen carefully. I am talking about the law, ancient law as it concerned women. In a farming community, it was considered sinful to let a field lie fallow, or a young widow go unmarried. Back then, by custom, the relative who took over the land would be expected to marry the widow (in this case, Ruth), or to marry her into his family, so there would be sons to compensate the dead man's family. The land would be worked and harvested by the farmer who took over the land. However, when he died, the land would be left not to his other sons, but to the boy who was descended from the original owner."

"To Ruth's baby, Mr. Eliot's grandson!" crowed Rosy, triumphantly.

"Well, not exactly," said Daisy, wrinkling her brow. "Hilion was already dead and even if Ruth married this second cousin, her child would not be Mr. Eliot's *true* grandson. She wasn't Mr. Eliot's true daughter, nor Naomi's . . ." She stopped, confused.

"But close enough," said Sylvania. "Hilion's wife would be the mother of a child from Naomi's husband's family, which was the best Naomi could hope for."

"What if Ruth didn't want to marry Mr. Second Cousin?" asked Rosie.

"What if Mr. Second Cousin decided not to marry Ruth?" asked Daisy.

"That's exactly what happened," said Sylvania. "He thought it over and decided that he didn't want to put all those years of work into plowing and planting what was not very good land, only to hand it over a generation later to Mr. Eliot's heirs. He would rather sell it right away. Besides (the great-aunts never told me this; I am seeing her clearly for the first time), Ruth was not pretty! She had always been poor; she had worked all her life. She had suffered a long journey and grueling hardship in the fields. She had lost some teeth, her skin was weathered, her hands scarred. Her hair was like a cowpat. And she wasn't young any more. Young enough to bear a child, but not *young* young."

"She probably owned only one dress," said Daisy, sympathizing.

"And that awful old shawl with bits of food on it," said Rosy. "Yuk!"

"Harvest was almost over, so there was going to be a festival. Everyone would be going to the dance, but Ruth didn't want to go."

"She thought she was too ugly," said Daisy. "And she had absolutely nothing to wear."

"Like Cinderella," said Rosy.

"Naomi insisted that she go anyway," said Sylvania. "She washed Ruth's skirt and blouse and brushed her shawl with fuller's earth to make it clean as she could. Then she brought more water for a bath and helped Ruth wash her hair and comb it out. Even so, Naomi had to push her daughter-in-law out the door."

"She was being the fairy godmother," said Rosy.

"When Ruth got to the grange hall, no one asked her to dance. She found herself sitting on a bench in the shadows, feeling alone and awkward. Then she noticed that Mr. Boaz was sitting in the shadow, too, in a corner of the settle. He was startled but pleased to discover that she was sitting next to him. They got to talking, Ruth and Mr. Boaz, and she found it was as easy to talk to him as it was to Naomi. It was like those good times in the old house in Moab, when she and Oprah and Malcolm and Hilion had talked and told stories and laughed. Mr. Boaz had a wonderful rich laugh. He reminded her of Hilion, but he was older and wiser. So was she, after all that had happened to her.

"For the first time since she had come to Brighouse, Ruth found someone who was interested in where she had come from, and how she felt about living so far away from her people. Mr. Boaz asked her about crops and herds in Moab, about soil conditions. He listened fascinated as she told him about laws concerning water rights in a land where there was not much water. They talked about trade and trade routes; she described to him not only the usual trade in grain and cattle, but cargoes of silk and perfume and spices she had seen go through her village.

" 'They'd be bound for Macclesfield,' said Mr. Boaz. Then he asked her how the Moabites celebrated their harvest.

"Usually Ruth was closemouthed about such things, but

now she found herself telling Squire Boaz (the most powerful man in the neighborhood!) how her family and the other people of her village danced along the road in procession, carrying honey cakes and fruits. When they came near a shrine, they walked into the field to where there was a statue of one of the local goddesses. There they did honor with songs and prayers: they splashed wine on the statue's feet and left an offering of cakes and special apples called pomegranates.

"Mr. Boaz did not seem shocked or angry about what she had told him. Indeed, he listened with open mouth. She rushed to tell him that she had promised Naomi that she would follow Naomi's god and Naomi's ways. And she did! She went to service every Sabbath; she found more to think about in Naomi's religion than she ever had in her own. But it was such a comfort to be able to talk to someone who was

not upset when she spoke of where and how she used to live. Mr. Boaz fell silent, lost in thought. Then he roused himself: 'Bless my soul! You should be out there on the grange floor dancing with the young folk. Don't spend all your time with an old man like me.'

" 'I don't know how to dance very well,' Ruth said. This was not exactly true. What she meant was that when in Moab, she had danced in a different way, barefoot in the dust, to the sound of flutes and tinkling cymbals. In Yorkshire, men and women hopped and stomped about on the dance floor, holding on to each other for dear life, making a raucous racket with their boots as the fiddlers sawed out raucous tunes. In Moab, the women danced as Gypsies do, with their whole bodies. Their movements were sinuous and silent, like a barley field when the wind ripples through.

" 'I don't dance very well either,' Mr. Boaz mused. 'I was always the squire's son and now I'm the squire. Girls are either afraid to dance with me and don't talk, or they are too eager to dance with me and talk too much. Thank goodness for my gimpy leg. Now I have an excuse not to get out there and make a fool of myself.'

"Ruth knew with all her heart and mind that she didn't want to spend time dancing with young folk, nor with any other folk for that matter. She would rather spend every precious moment she could with Mr. Boaz because –"

"Because she was falling in love with him," said Daisy and Rosy together.

"And he was falling in love with her. They talked all night long. Well, not *all* night. In the morning he asked her to marry him. Now it was the custom for the prettiest girl at the dance to be made the Barley Queen, and she was given a corn dolly, made from stalks of the last sheaf cut, as a prize for being pretty. The other people, including the Barley Queen, had all long gone home, when Mr. Boaz picked up some stalks that were lying on the grange floor. . . ."

"He was *gleaning*!" cried Rosy.

"So he could make a corn dolly for Ruth. She had not imagined such patience and skill existed in the man! He coaxed those stalks into shape: he braided them, tied them, and at the end of it all, a little barley-straw lady was standing on the palm of his outstretched hand."

"I bet she had a long neck with almost no head," said Rosy, "like the corn dolls you and Father make for us. He says the long neck is her husband."

"I bet she was wearing a skirt with thirteen grain heads for panels," said Daisy. "One for each of the thirteen moons of the year. Like *you* always show us."

"Then Mr. Boaz took Ruth's hand and led her out into the center of the empty grange hall. 'Look ye, lads and lasses all!' he boomed into the empty stillness. 'Here's for my own dear Queen of the Barley, awarded her for being the kindest, bravest, most intelligent woman from Brighouse to Moab.'"

"And then he kissed her," said Rosy, hopefully.

"Yes, he did. And now I'll kiss both of you," said Sylvania. "Good night. Go to sleep. I'm all storied out."

CHAPTER 4

THE STRANGER

AS SUMMER DWINDLED into fall, Sylvania left the girls to tend the hut, the garden, and the yard while she hastened to glean as much as she could before the onset of winter. Now she collected nuts and haws and rose hips. She picked dry teasels to sell to weavers, and sought ale-hoof root to sell to brewers. She also dug for mandrake root, harvested honey from the wild bees, and gathered mushrooms of various kinds.

The most important skill Sylvania had learned from her grandmothers and aunts was how to practice medicine. People came from a long way away to ask her advice about aches and fevers, and to pay for pills and poultices. But what Sylvania the Forest Wife was most famous for was her ability to cure wounds. She kept a colony of maggots to use against axe wounds, and for festering sores brought back from the war. She knew the benefit of spiderwebs for curing infection. She also sold leeches, along with advice on how to use them for bruises and for bloodletting. She still ached for Bernardo, but she did not talk about him as much as she used to. Daisy and Rosy forgot to play the "I Remember" game.

Sylvania was away so much that Daisy had taken over most of the spinning, as well as the sewing and the cooking. Rosy, in addition to her other duties, learned to sort the herbs and to dry them on wooden racks she had devised and made. She fashioned little birch bark boxes in which to store dried roots, dried leaves, and seeds.

Sometimes a neighbor woman came to the door to buy a packet of mint or chamomile, a basket of blackberries, or a jar of forest honey. Young as they were, the girls were quite capable of taking the coins, making change, and marking the sale in the ruled account book. When someone they didn't know, or whom their mother didn't trust, came a-knocking they would call through the keyhole: "Sorry, the shop is closed." The heavy oaken door, built by Bernardo, was strong and well made, as was the oaken bar. Hasp, lock, and hinges were forged from iron.

One day, when Rosy was working in the garden, she saw a creature come shambling out of the woods. It looked for all the world like an upright bear. As the creature came nearer on the path, she saw it was a man, a man with a face so dirty you could have planted watercress in the creases of his skin. He was leaning on a staff. His beard was filthy and his filthy hair looked as though it had not been washed or combed or cut for a century. As he came closer, Rosy saw the huge dirty toes sticking out of the man's boots. The boots stuck to his black ankles like a second skin. His layers of clothing looked more like greenish fur than any kind of cloth.

The stranger came up to the gate, rattled it, and gave a strange cry. Rosy caught a whiff from his body that made her stomach churn. Gagging and choking she ran for the hut, dashed through the door, and shut it with a bang. Daisy, who had heard the door slam, rushed to help her shove the heavy oaken bar through the iron hasps. They turned the key in the lock and ran to latch the windows. They clung together, holding their breaths, as they listened to the man-creature prowling and growling around the house.

"I know you're in there," he shouted. "Tell her I came!" They watched him stumble down the path and into the woods.

At sunset, when their mother came home, they told her all that had happened. Sylvania listened carefully and made them tell the story over and over, questioning them about every detail. That night she set a lamp in the window and sent the girls up to the loft early. They heard her pacing the floor below them all night long.

When morning came, Sylvania did not go into the Forest to work. Instead, she dragged her biggest tub out to the shed in the yard. She built a fire under the cauldron in the kitchen, and filled it full of water. She set Rosy to pumping water into every pail and bowl and pitcher they owned, while she and Daisy lined them up near the hearth. She laid out towels, soap, scissors on the tool bench in the shed, and she searched in the clothes chest that stood at the foot of her bed. She brought out an old shirt and a pair of trousers that had belonged to Bernardo.

At last she called her children to her. "I have been walking and thinking all night," she said, "and I have concluded that the man you saw yesterday is your father. He is Bernardo come home from the wars."

"You're wrong!" shouted Rosy.

"He couldn't be!" wailed Daisy. "You should have seen him. He was disgusting."

"He stinks!" said Rosy, and burst into tears.

Sylvania sighed. Sylvania waited. She waited for three days. Then up the path he came again, that man who looked like a bear. This time he tramped up to the gate, halted, called out an order to himself, saluted. He called out another order, shouldered his staff like a musket, whirled it about, presented arms. Then he called: "Sylvania! It's me! Bernardo!"

She ran to him. She ran and would have thrown her arms around him, but he backed away. "No," he said. "I'm disgusting. I stink. Let me have a bath."

She pointed to the shed and brought out a pitcher of hot water. She helped him cut the clothes off his body and the shoes from his feet. Rosy, meanwhile, worked the pump and carried water into the kitchen. Daisy staggered back and forth with vessels full of hot water. Sylvania would not let the girls enter the shed.

Sylvania emptied the tub over and over again, and called

for more hot water. She cut her husband's beard and she cut his hair, washing and combing as she worked. Finally he toweled himself and put on his shirt and trousers. A pair of old boots stood waiting for him, near the door. He stepped out into the yard, blinking.

Daisy and Rosy blinked, too. This was not the father they remembered, certainly not the father whose triumphant return they had so vividly imagined. This man was smaller than Bernardo had been when he went off to war. Or perhaps he only seemed so because they had grown bigger.

Bernardo was so bone weary he tottered, and so thin that he had to tie his trousers with a cord wrapped twice around his waist. There was a scar on his face that ran down by his nose to one corner of his mouth; his lip drooped slightly. Despite the many scrubbings, his face still seemed ingrained with dirt. As he moved toward them, they saw he limped a little.

"Well, don't just stand there," he said. "Aren't you going to give your father a hug?"

Hesitantly, they moved toward him, submitted to being drawn within the circle of his arms. They could feel the bones beneath his skin. He was more like a goat than a bear. He smelled like a goat, too. They stood still, politely, while he pressed them to his bony chest. As soon as he released them, they went to stand by Sylvania.

At dinnertime they watched as their father stuffed his mouth with bread and cheese; they recoiled as he picked up the bowl and slurped down the last of the soup. He told them, while his mouth was full, that when he had come to the hut a few days before, he had concluded that strangers had taken over the house. He could hardly believe that the two tall girls he glimpsed through the windows were his own little girls. The garden had looked different and so had the goats; he did not even recognize the hens. Now he saw that the inside of the house had been turned into an apothecary shop.

"That will all go," he told Sylvania, "as soon as I get my job back. I'll sort things out with Huw tomorrow. He'll know the lay of the land."

Next day he hunted out his axe and sharpened it. He went off confidently to seek his old friends. But the news was not good. "Now that the soldiers have come back from the war," said Huw, "the king has more men than trees. We spent years cutting down the Forest for him, and now he doesn't know what to do with us."

"And we don't know what to do with ourselves," said Bernardo.

Bernardo busied himself about the hut. He attacked the garden as though it were the enemy. He dug about aimlessly, displacing the rows of kale and potatoes that Rosy had set out. He decided to fix the pots and pans, and left a dent in Daisy's favorite copper kettle. He was impatient with the amount of space taken up by the drying racks, and seemed almost deliberately careless when he brushed by them, disturbing their delicate balance. He resented the time that Sylvania spent in the Forest, yet he refused to go with her. "All that gleaning and gathering!" he said. "That's woman's work."

Every night the girls gave their father a dutiful kiss on the cheek. After their first cold reception, he never again tried to hug them; instead, he sought every way he could to belittle them and their efforts. He didn't lay a hand on his wife or daughters; he never once hit them. But, lying in their beds in the loft, the girls could hear their parents quarreling. Sometimes, when everything was quiet, they were awakened by a cry of horror in the night, and they heard their mother's voice, trying to soothe him. When daylight came, Bernardo complained constantly that Sylvania had changed, and not for the better. "Where has my sweet little girl gone?" they heard him ask more than once.

"I never was your little girl and I never will be," became Sylvania's standard reply. "I'm as grown up as you are. Maybe more so."

He, a woodsman, strong as a bear, had gone away as a

veritable prince of a man. His nature, then, had been generous, good-humored, and loving. Alas! On the battlefield a poisonous barb had entered near Bernardo's heart. He came back diminished in body and soul. He found fault with everything and could never be satisfied. When Sylvania asked him to keep shop while she and the girls went a-gleaning, he whined (yes, Bernardo actually whined): "What? I'll be a laughing-stock. Everyone will know what a henpecked husband I am."

More than once, exasperated, Sylvania found herself shouting at him: *"Stop being henpecked!"*

"There! See? You just proved what I've been telling you," he would say. She didn't know whether to laugh or cry. Almost every day now, Bernardo flung out of the house and went off to the nearest town to drink and gamble with Huw and his other old army mates. Sometimes he didn't come home at night.

When they weren't arguing, Sylvania did her best to please and placate her husband, until she blew up again. The distance widened between them. He paid less and less attention to her, and almost no attention to Daisy and Rosy. Like a departing traveler seen on a heath from far off, he dwindled in the offing. Eventually he was gone for days and weeks. Despite all her knowledge, all her vast collection of medicines, and her reputation for healing wounds, Sylvania the Forest Wife had no cure for what ailed her own husband.

Weeks passed before they had news of him. Sylvania grieved when she heard that Bernardo had gone to work in the mine tunnels. Months later she grieved more when she heard that he had re-emerged from the mines and was living in town. Rumor had it that he lived on money made from nefarious trades.

Sylvania was desperate. In all her store of knowledge, in all the lore her grandmothers had taught her, there was neither word nor potion nor healing art that she could use to cure her husband's wound. *Desperate circumstances call for desperate measures!* She and her daughters would go to seek the Green Knight and ask him how to bring back the husband and father who was now lost to them. "Just as we are wise in the ways of women," her grandmothers had told her, "the Green Knight is wise in the ways of men."

Sylvania had never before been to where the Green Knight lives, nor did she know anyone who had. On the last page of her mother's commonplace book, there was a map. It showed roads, footpaths, rivers, and landmarks that led to the chapel of the Green Knight. The journey was arduous. Along the margins of the map, her mother had written a warning: *To be undertaken only in need most dire.*

The journey to-and-fro would take more than a week. Sylvania and her daughters must follow Dane River into Wildboarclough, a place hid amidst awful peaks and rocks. When they had almost reached their goal, they would hear a roar, coming from the rapids where Black Brook joins Dane River. Just beyond would be a green hill, or mound. Long, long ago the hill had swollen up like a bubble in a porridge pot and blown its top. Now its flanks were covered with wide-branching trees that concealed both the hole at the top and the hollowness below. *The Green Knight lived in that hollow hill.*

The Forest Family walked and walked, following the grandmothers' map and directions. On the third day, they heard a roar and saw where the peat-darkened foam of Black Brook rushes to meet the silvery rapids of Dane River. Beyond, just as promised, lay a small rounded hill so perfect in its symmetry that it looked man-made.

They crossed the torrent on a single-log bridge, then they followed the path that wound in a spiral 'round the hill. At last they came to a crack in the hillside and found themselves peering down into a rocky hollow, a sort of grotto. Moss and lichen covered the rocks with a greenish cast. Ferny tufts and spindly trees grew from clefts in the rugged walls, so that emerald light was filtered down from the hole at the top. A thick carpet of green moss covered the steps that led down into the cavern. At the bottom of the steps was a green man, very old.

This, Sylvania knew, was the Green Knight. His skin was greenish, his hair pale green. Ragged green silks and mildewed furs were held together by a vine of ivy wrapped about his waist; he was patched all over with thorn-pierced leaves. He was bending over a pot, which looked suspiciously like a battered helmet; he was stirring something with a broken axe. Both helm and axe were rimed with verdigris. He did not look up at them as they approached.

"So you have come at last," he said.

"I have come," said Sylvania, "to ask you how to bring

back my man." She told the Green Knight how her husband had gone off to war, how a poisonous barb had lodged near his heart, and how he no longer behaved like the man she remembered. The Green Knight turned to look at her.

"Ah," he said, "I know all there is to know of war, and I know too well about the men who return from there. Some come back the better for their experience; many come back the worse."

Sylvania opened her mouth, about to speak, but the Green Knight gave her no opening. "Listen to me," he said. "The greatest bully in the world is a henpecked husband. The most boring person in the world is a so-sorry-for-herself wife." He turned away from her again. "Go home," he said, over his shoulder. "You're boring me."

But Sylvania would not go home, not yet anyway. She and her daughters set up camp among the rocks. Every day, with her daughters watching and hanging on her words, she asked the Green Knight to tell her how she could get her man back, the man she remembered. She pleaded with him to concoct a potion, to teach her the spell that would make it work. The knight seemed not to listen, nor even to notice her.

Then one day Daisy and Rosy, unbidden, spoke out.

"Tell our mother what she needs to bring back her husband," said Rosy.

"Tell us what we must do to bring back our father," said Daisy.

"Teach us the magic spell," they said together.

CHAPTER 5

BEAR'S WHISKER, GNOME'S BEARD

FOR THE FIRST TIME, the Green Knight turned to take a good look at them. "I don't believe in spells. Nor magic," he said. "Oh, I can tell you and your mother to bring me a rare and special something. Oh, I can concoct and mutter and wave my hands three times three. But such things never work, not even if the users are brave and clever."

"We *are* brave and clever," said Sylvania. "Tell us what to do."

The Green Knight sighed. "First, get on with your life. Second, stop being sorry for yourself. Then, before any hocus-pocus can happen, you will have to bring me three hairs from a bear's lip. A wild bear. A live bear. And those hairs must be plucked by your own hand."

"I can do that," she said, not flinching.

The Green Knight sighed again and peered straight into her eyes. "Perhaps you can," he said, "but the next part is harder. Each of your daughters would have to bring me a tuft from the same source."

"We can do that," said Daisy and Rosy. But their mother turned pale.

❦

When Sylvania returned to her own house, she did not speak to her daughters about potions or spells, and forbade Daisy and Rosy to talk about them, too. But one night when there was a full moon and her daughters were asleep, she went up into the hills behind her house, to a place of rocks and caves. She had heard from old hunters that once a bear had lived there.

"Bear," she called, "are you listening? I have brought you a present." And she left a piece of honeycomb on the rock in front of a cave. When next she came that way, she noticed that the honeycomb was gone. A few nights later she went up the hill again. "Bear," she said, "listen to me. I will come almost every night and bring you a bowl of milk and honey. In return I ask that you show yourself to me."

Week after week went by. Every few nights the Forest Wife went up into the hills to bring milk and honey, and to speak to the bear. One night she thought she saw his eyes gleaming at the back of the cave. A month went by and the moon was full again. She stood below the mouth of the cave and looked up as she called. "Bear, here is your honey." Then she saw, not the bear, but the shadow of the bear, silhouetted on the rocks, in the moonlight.

Another month went by. Now when she went to the cave, the bear would be waiting for her. Every night he let her draw closer and closer. At last she drew so close that he came the few steps forward and ate from the bowl she held in her hands. The next night she put out a hand and touched his great head as he ate. She rubbed and scratched his thick fur, but when she touched an old wound behind one of his ears, he gave such a growl that she dropped the bowl and ran down the hill.

She went back again. Even though she had to start all over, almost from the beginning, she persisted. At last came a time when she could say, "Bear, I ask your forgiveness. I need three hairs from your lip." Then – quick, quick, quick – she drew them out. She put the hairs in her apron pocket and ran down the hill, never looking behind her. A few nights later she returned (to apologize to the bear), but she saw no sign of him. The cave was empty. When winter came she told herself to forget him. But she put the hairs into a box of carved rosewood and set it high on a shelf. She sighed as she remembered how Bernardo had carved the box for her when they were still sweethearts.

When spring came again, Daisy and Rosy went to run outdoors. One day, while they were playing at the edge of the
meadow, they thought they heard the sound of an axe in the
woods. The sound was so slight, they agreed, that either the
woodsman was very far off, or he was using a very small axe.
They went together to investigate when, suddenly, they heard
cries and shouts for help. Rushing forward they came upon a
clearing. A long-nosed gnome with a long wispy beard was
dancing about and shrieking as though in agony. Rosy could
see at a glance what had happened: the little man had par-
tially split a birch log, and placed a wedge in it in order to cut
the wood more easily. When next he struck, the wedge flew
out, the log sprang shut, and the tip of his long, long beard
was trapped in a wooden vice. Pull his beard and dance about
as he might, the gnome could not free himself.

"Well, don't just stand there, you ninnies. *Do* something!" he yelled.

Rosy ran to pry the log apart and Daisy tried to persuade
the gnome to calm himself, but he would not stand still. All
the time, as he jumped about, he was hurling insults and
curses at them, accusing them of clumsiness and of enjoying
his predicament.

"You are just trying to steal my gold," he screamed. For
the first time the girls noticed a long leather bag full of gold
coins lying nearby. At that moment Rosy reached into her
pocket and withdrew her trusty penknife. In a trice she had
cut off the tip of the gnome's wispy beard. The gnome gave

a scream of anguish, then rushed to pick up the bag. As he tied it to his belt he cried, "You wicked, raw-faced wench! You have sapped my strength and made me the laughing-stock of the whole world!" So saying, he scuttled away into the underbrush.

The girls went home and told their mother the story of what had happened. Sylvania listened carefully. When they showed her the wisps of hair that Rosy had cut from the tip of the gnome's beard, she asked if she could have them. She put the hairs into the same carved wooden box where she had put the three hairs plucked from the lip of the bear.

When summer came, the girls asked their mother if they could go down to the stream to fish. As they approached the rushing waters, they heard some pitiful squeaks and saw that something was thrashing about in the reeds. Thinking that it might be a wounded otter, they rushed forward to see if they could help. To their astonishment, they beheld the little man again. He, too, had decided to take rod and line that day, and had actually hooked a trout – a big one. Silver and green, stippled with rose moles, it was hauled half out of the water. The trouble was that as the fish took the bait, the gnome's beard had become entangled in the fishing line; he was being dragged down the bank. The fish was bigger than the gnome, and so powerful that it was pulling him into the river. To give credit where credit is due, the gnome was resisting with every ounce of his puny strength. He had dug in his heels, but all that resulted were two tiny ruts

being plowed in the mud as he was dragged closer and closer to death by drowning.

The girls rushed forward to help. Rosy took the gnome's shoulders and tried to pull him back from the bank whilst he struggled as much against her as against the fish. "Unhand me, you unnatural hulking creatures!" he yelled, as Rosy pulled and Daisy sought to untangle his beard. "You've been spying on me again, just waiting to get my pearls." For the first time, the girls noticed a leather bag lying half open from whence a wealth of pearls was spilling. At that moment, Daisy reached into her pocket and withdrew a pair of sewing scissors. Swiftly she snipped the beard at its very tip and freed the little man just as the fish dove deep. The gnome fell back into the mud and lay there for a moment, sputtering. Then he scrambled up the bank and grabbed the bag of pearls. "You can't fool me, cottage cheese face," he snarled. "I know what you're up to. You're whittling my beard away so you can steal all my power!" Then he darted into the reeds.

The girls went home and told the story to their mother. Sylvania listened carefully. When they showed her the wisps from the gnome's beard, she asked if she might have them. Then she put them into the rosewood coffer along with the other hairs and placed the box high on a shelf.

❦

Autumn came. Sylvania took her daughters into the Forest to glean nuts and rose hips and the last of the year's richness. That task done, she told the girls to be prepared to go with her to pay a second call on the Green Knight. She would take him the hairs in the rosewood coffer and ask him to make the right potion, teach her the right spell. The sky was dark as they traveled. Toward the end of their journey, they were beset by a storm. Sleet was on the wind. They had to inch their way across the icy log that spanned Black Brook. At the base of the hollow hill, they pulled their cloaks close before they wound up the spiral path. Daisy's teeth were chattering. "Keep moving," said Sylvania. "As long as we keep going, we won't freeze."

"The snot in my nose is frozen," Rosy reported.

When they came to the crack in the hillside, they descended frost-slicked steps and found themselves once again in the green grotto. The Green Knight was still bending over his rusty helmet, still stirring something with his broken axe, just as though they had never left him. The only difference was that now the trees above him were bare of leaves. There was no emerald light sifting down through the leaves, but the rocks were still green with lichen. Moss and ferns grew on every ledge. A bough of holly was propped against the cliff, within hand's reach of the Green Knight.

"Aha!" he said, without bothering to look over his shoulder. "So you've come at last."

"We've been here before," said the Forest Wife, somewhat tartly. "It is I, Sylvania, and my two daughters, Daisy and Rosy."

The Green Knight whipped 'round to take a look at them. His pale green eyebrows shot up. "It's *you*!" he said. "What are you doing here? No one ever comes back to see me a second time."

"I've come to bring what you told me to bring," said Sylvania.

"I don't remember," mumbled the old knight, and he turned back to his stirring. Then, over his shoulder: "I never told you to bring me anything. What would I want from the likes of you?"

"You told me to bring three hairs from a bear's lip," said Sylvania. "Now you can use them to concoct that potion. You will teach me the spell that goes with it and I will have my man back again. And my children will have their father."

"I never promised you any such nonsense," said the Green Knight. "Besides," he said, turning to look at her,

cunningly, "I said each of your daughters must bring hairs from the same source."

"They are all here, in this box," said Sylvania. And she held out the intricately carved coffer.

"Give it me," said the Green Knight. He peered into the

box; poked at the hairs with a gnarled finger. Sylvania watched him warily.

"I want to be honest with you," she confessed. "Only three of the hairs come from a bear. The rest are from a gnome's beard."

"Knew that!" snapped the Green Knight. "Bear's whisker, gnome's beard; bear's beard, gnome's whisker. No difference. All the same. How did you get these things?"

So Sylvania told him her story about the bear. She told him how the bear had allowed her to come closer and closer, and how at last she had petted him. She told him how she had touched an old wound and how she had to start over again, almost from the beginning. Then she told him how she had plucked the three hairs and run down the hill, very fast.

The Green Knight listened carefully, all the time rolling the wad of hair into a smaller and tighter ball until it was the size of a pill. When she was done, there was a long silence. She wondered if she should tell him Rosy's and Daisy's stories about the gnome, but he did not ask. At last he placed the ball of hair between his finger and thumb, looked at it inquiringly, *and threw it into the fire.* In a blink of an eye, flames flared up and consumed what had taken so much effort to win. All hope was dashed.

Sylvania gave an anguished cry. "You promised!" she said. "You promised to make me that potion. You promised to teach me the spell!"

"I promised nothing," said the Green Knight. "Woman,

listen to me! If you can make friends with a wild beast, you don't need potions and spells."

"But how can I make my husband change?" asked Sylvania.

"You can't. He's the only one who can do that. And I'll tell you something else: Your man can't make you happy. You are the only one who can do that."

"You're mean," said Rosy.

"You're not playing fair," said Daisy.

"We just want to have a happy family," wailed Rosy.

"Like everybody else," Daisy whimpered.

"So? So, the three of you are already, most of the time, a happy family. Granted, your family may not be absolutely perfect," said the Green Knight. Then he roared: "BUT IT'S GOOD ENOUGH!"

His words echoed and re-echoed, bouncing and booming off the walls of the rocky grotto. Sylvania and her daughters stood gaping at him until, softly and precisely, he said, "Go home. Stop bothering me. Learn to live with what you've got."

CHAPTER 6

A QUESTION AND AN ANSWER

WHEN THEY REACHED home again, Sylvania did not speak about what had happened and she forbade her daughters to do so. Winter closed in around them.

One stormy night the Forest Family sat before the fire. Sylvania was poring over her mother's commonplace book. The writing was so crabbed that she had difficulty deciphering it. After long silence, she spoke: "This part may interest you, Daisy. It tells about how to make thread from nettles. The art must be very ancient. I've never heard about it before."

"Except in fairy tales," said Daisy. "Remember the story where seven princes were turned into seven swans and a maiden wove seven shirts of nettle to save them? But there weren't quite enough for the youngest prince –"

"Who would want to wear nettles?" asked Rosy, scornfully.

"According to my mother's book, the aunts and grand-mothers said there is a trick to making the thread," said Sylvania. "You have to move your hand *up* the stalk. The stingers should lie flat and be quite comfortable to handle." Rosy still looked so doubtful that Sylvania felt called upon to defend the idea. "It says right here that thread made out of nettles is finer and stronger than thread made from flax."

"How would I make such thread?" asked Daisy, suddenly eager.

"Well, first you gather the nettles. Then you spread the stalks out to dry. After that you soak them in water, so the outer part rots away. Inside each stalk is a long stringy pith –"

Just then came a knock at the door. Rosie sprang up to open it. She lifted the wooden bar from the haft and slid it aside, then she pulled the handle. As the door swung open, a huge bear shambled into the room and dropped down onto the hearth rug. His coat was covered with ice and snow. Rosy ran for a broom to sweep his coat clean; Daisy poured him a pail of warm milk and honey so that he might be given strength. The bear was so exhausted, they let him stay the night.

In the morning the storm still raged, so they did not drive the bear away. That night by the fire he seemed so contented and harmless that the girls began to play with him. They pushed and shoved him and rolled him from side to side. They began to tease him and to take liberties with his strength, but when they had gone too far, or were too familiar, he gave a warning growl, though he seemed good-natured enough. When they told stories, and when Sylvania read aloud from the leather-bound book, he seemed to listen with as much attention as they. That night Sylvania let him stay again. The three of them became so used to his presence, and he to theirs, that they let him come and go all winter long. He had become a friend, a welcome guest in the hut. He was almost like a member of the family.

One cold clear night between Christmas and New Year's, the bear lay on the hearth, snoring gently. Rosy roused herself enough to say, "Aren't there any *other* Christmas stories?"

"Christmas is over," yawned Daisy. "I want a New Year's story."

"There used to be a story that my father told every year on the day after Christmas," said Sylvania. "It's about King Arthur. The King Arthur stories were always told by a man, but since there is no male in our household. . . ."

"Except for Bear," Daisy corrected.

"I'll do my best to tell it to you anyway."

"Wake up, Bear," said Rosy. "This is a story especially for you."

"Of all the knights of King Arthur's court the youngest, the handsomest, the most impetuous was his own nephew, Sir Gawain. Now this particular Christmas, King Arthur decided to keep Christmas at Castle Carlisle, on the northern border. The day *after* Christmas, King Arthur, jaded by too many Yuletide festivities, decided to ride out on quest.

"All through the silvery Forest of Islington he rode, where every trunk and branch and twig was sheathed in ice that sparkled in the winter sun. At last he came to the very center of the Forest; there he found a deep dark pool, Tarn Watling by name. Thick ice penetrated its very depths. On the encircling banks lay ferns and withered sedge, frosted with hoar. On the other side of the tarn there was a castle, a moated place with walls and towers. King Arthur called out a challenge. His challenge was answered. The portcullis went up, the drawbridge went down, and out rode a giant knight. But it was not his size alone that astonished. This knight was gorgeous, glittering green!"

"Green?" squealed Daisy and Rosy together.

"His skin was green, his clothes were green, his horse was green, his armor was green. His helmet, which he had not yet donned, was cradled in the crook of one arm, almost like a head. He rode 'round one edge of the tarn; King Arthur rode toward him 'round the other. As they came closer, King Arthur looked and looked again, increasingly aware that the Green Knight's green hair fell in curls down his back; that it sprouted like vine tendrils from his ears and

from the corners of his mouth. *And* that his eyebrows were like tufts of emerald moss.

"Hastily King Arthur went to pull his sword from its scabbard, but it was as though frozen. He tried to lower the point of his lance, but it would not budge. And all the time the giant knight was bearing down upon him. 'Aha!' that giant knight cried out, 'Now I have you in my power! I will see you thrust into the deepest, darkest dungeon in all the land.' He grabbed Arthur's sword and lance, and threw them clattering onto the frozen pond. Then *he* looked and looked again. 'But you are King Arthur! King Arthur himself! For you I will give special dispensation. If you will return to this place within three days – with the answer to my question – I shall allow you to go free. But if you *cannot* answer, I shall treat you like any ordinary knight.'

" 'What,' asked King Arthur, '*what* is the question?'

" 'The question is,' said the Green Knight, 'the question is: *What does a woman really want?*' "

"Look at Bear!" said Rosy, excitedly. For the bear, who had been lying half-asleep on the hearth rug, now shivered from head to toe and opened both eyes wide.

"He's looking at *you*," Daisy said, speaking to Sylvania.

"Maybe he knows the answer," said Rosy, hopefully. At which the bear gave such a growl that she jumped back into the depths of her chair.

"Or maybe he doesn't," said Sylvania. "Where was I? Oh, yes! *'What does a woman really want?'*

" 'That,' said King Arthur, 'is a hard question.' As cheerily as he had ridden out in the morn, now wearily, wearily he turned back toward Castle Carlisle. That night in the great hall he sat at the high table with his queen, Guinevere, on one side of him and his nephew-heir, young Gawain, on the other. Knights and ladies, according to their rank, sat at long tables below them. Rich broth was carried in and served from great silver bowls. Fowl and fish and venison were carved, pickled herbs and black puddings were shared, and there was brown

beer and bright wine aplenty for the quaffing. Because this was still Yuletide, gifts were being exchanged and, under the mistletoe, kisses stolen. Laughter and good talk held sway.

"When the boards were being cleared and the sweets brought forth, some of the knights called out for an accounting of King Arthur's quest. Others joined in, rattling their runcible spoons against bowls and goblets: 'The quest! The quest! King Arthur's quest!' they shouted.

"So King Arthur told them of his adventure – of the silvery wood and the dark tarn and the Green Knight. When his own knights heard of the threat to throw him into a dungeon, many offered to go in his stead. But King Arthur said: 'No. It was my quest. I am a true knight. I shall return to Tarn Watling three days hence, just as I promised. But you can help me answer the question. Come now, noble knights! What do you think a woman really wants?'

" 'Oh, that's easy,' said Sir Lionel. 'A woman wants gold and jewels.'

" 'She wants a bunch of violets,' said Sir Lancelot.

" 'She wants silks and spices and perfumes from the East,' said Sir Perceval.

" 'She wants good boats and strong nets and men who know how to use them,' said King Lot. Lot was king of the Orkneys and Gawain's father to boot. Curiously, Sir Gawain said nothing. For once he kept his mouth shut.

" 'She *should* want pigs and cattle, fields and houses,' said Sir Bevedere, 'and a sensible husband to guide her.'

" 'She wants a young lover,' said Tristan.

" 'No, no, no!' protested Sir Galahad, shocked. 'She wants a husband, children, a virtuous reputation.'

"Somehow King Arthur felt that none of these sufficed, but on the third morn he cantered out once more, through the shining wood. Riding deeper into the wilderness, so immersed in thought was he that he did not hear a voice cry out, 'What doth ail thee, knight-at-arms?' He rode on a little bit further and the voice cried out again, 'What doth ail thee, knight-at-arms?' He pulled up his horse and looked about. There on a log, 'twixt oak and holly, sat the ugliest woman he ever saw. He knew at once, without introduction, that she was Lady Ragnall, the Winter Hag.

"Dumpy and squat, yet dressed all in scarlet was she. One eye was up here, one was down there. Her nose was pulled one way, her chin the other. Her skin was rough and grooved as the bark of an oak. Her arms were like boughs of trees, her hands like spans of twig. Her ankles writhed like the roots of old trees out of her scarlet shoes. Ever courteous, King Arthur tried not to notice that her sprung buttocks spread all over the log. Quite sweetly she repeated, 'What doth ail thee, knight-at-arms?'

"King Arthur told her. He told her about his quest and the Green Knight and the Green Knight's threat to throw him into a dungeon unless he answered a certain difficult question. When he, on her behest, repeated the question, she exclaimed, 'I know the answer to that! The Green Knight is my twin brother. We are like two sides of the same coin; what he knows, I know. Lean down and I will whisper certain secret words into your ear. But take care! Tell no one what I say to you. If my answer proves, promise to give to me whatever I ask for when you come this way again.'

" 'Of course, of course, dear lady,' said King Arthur, thinking, *What could this loathly lady ever want? A bracelet, a bangle, a length of scarlet silk?* He leaned down from his horse and allowed the hag to put her loathsome lips to his ear – *although I must admit he closed his eyes* – whilst she whispered certain words to him. Eager to pursue his quest, King Arthur barely thanked her, then spurred his horse forward into the greenwood. When he came to the tarn, he called out a challenge. His challenge was answered. The portcullis went up, the drawbridge came down, and the Green Knight rode forth on his splendid steed.

" 'The question! The question! Answer the question!' he shouted. So King Arthur called out those words the Winter Hag had taught him. 'She told you! She told you! My sister told you!' the Green Knight screeched. Enraged, he wheeled his great green horse and clattered back to his castle. Gate chains rattled and the drawbridge closed behind him with a snap.

"Then King Arthur laughed out loud and long, his laughter echoing on the frosty air. Merrily he wended his way back to the Winter Hag. She was waiting for him, still sitting on a log 'twixt oak and holly. 'Aha!' she said. 'My words must have been the right ones for here you are before me, not languishing in a deep dark dungeon as seemed so likely short hours ago.'

" 'Indeed, dear Lady Ragnall,' said King Arthur. 'I cannot thank you enough. Pray tell me what you want and I will give it to you, just as I have promised.'

" 'I want,' said the Winter Hag sweetly, 'I want . . . the hand of Sir Gawain in marriage.'

"King Arthur turned red and white by turns. 'O Lady, Lady,' he protested, 'I cannot promise that. A knight cannot presume another knight's hand! Relent! Consider! Sir Gawain? He is so young, so handsome, so full of promise!'

" 'Nevertheless,' spake the awful hag, 'you made a knightly promise. Tell Sir Gawain what I have asked.'

"That night in the great hall, all were gathered to hear of the adventures of King Arthur. Strange as it may seem, although many had offered to go in place of King Arthur, to lie in the deepest darkest dungeon, no one offered to go in place of Sir Gawain, to lie in the bed of the Winter Hag.

"But Sir Gawain, listening (did I tell you he was impetuous?) said: 'I would see this Lady Ragnall.' And so next morning early, with silver bridles jingling, the knights went riding, riding, riding through the silvery Forest of Islington. When they came to the place where sat the Winter Hag, some knights stared and stared; some, out of knightly courtesy, turned aside; some went into the woods to puke. Sir Gawain, considering, saw how, despite her rambling shape, the lady hag sat upon her log with dignity and pride. Then (was he the only one?) he thought he saw a tear sparkle at the corner of one crooked eye. The next moment (did I ever happen to mention that Sir Gawain was impetuous?), he was down on his knees in the snow and had proposed!

"Now there was no help for it. Messengers were sent forward to Castle Carlisle to caution Queen Guinevere to prepare a marriage feast. Lady Ragnall was set up pillion to sit behind Sir Gawain on his horse. Somberly and soberly the knights rode back to the castle. No one would have guessed that they were celebrating a betrothal.

"I want you to listen carefully now, for there is something else you must know about Sir Gawain. His strength waxed and waned by day and by year. When he woke in the early hours, although young and lusty as he might appear, he was not yet as strong as he would be at midday. At noon he reached his zenith. As the hours waned, so did he, until at nightfall he was weak again. As with the day, so with the year. In January and February, he could barely lift a hand. Only in March did Sir Gawain's strength begin to return. In June, at summer solstice, it reached its height – on the longest day, the shortest night of the year. By September, though, he dwindled; he was no stronger than he had been in March. His powers slid down and down until the winter solstice – the shortest day and the longest night of the year. Then, his strength at lowest ebb, the tide began to turn."

"Just like you, Bear!" said Rosy. "*You* sleep all winter."

"Hush," said Daisy, "I want to hear the story."

"That night," continued Sylvania, "All were gathered for the marriage of Sir Gawain to the Winter Hag. I am sorry to report that the wine was flat, the music was flat, the jokes were flat, the stories were pointless. Acrobats came down with a thud; jugglers dropped whatever they were juggling. Hour after hour dragged by. Then it was almost midnight. Now the minutes went too fast! Alas! Time cannot be stayed. The moment came when king and queen must lead bride and groom up the long stairs, along the long gallery, to the door of the bridal chamber. The crowd followed, with much pushing and shoving, much craning of necks, many a drunken jest. Most knights and ladies pitied the handsome young groom; there were others who longed to witness his discomfiture. *Pity from one's own kind is worse than contempt.*

"Sir Gawain had to push the crowd away to reach the chamber door. He opened it just wide enough to let his lady pass through before him. Then he, too, slipped through the opening, shoved back the gawking crowd, closed the door, and slid the bar into place. When he turned again, he beheld the woman he had married. She was standing by a window. The moonlight shining through proved to him that she was as ugly as ever. But then Sir Gawain (you know Sir Gawain!) thought to himself, *She* is *my wedded wife*, and he went to her and kissed her – *although I must admit he closed his eyes.* When he opened them again, there stood a lady fair in form and face, encircled in his arms.

" 'Who . . . What?' stammered Sir Gawain.

" 'As you see me now,' said the lady, 'I am because you kissed me of your own free will upon our wedding night. But *because you closed your eyes*, I can be this way only half the time. So which would you rather? That I be:

Beautiful by day and Ugly by night,

or

Ugly by day and Beautiful by night?'

" 'Be as you are now! Be beautiful for me tonight,' said Sir Gawain. (You know Sir Gawain!) 'Let the day take care of itself!' But the lady shook her head sadly.

" 'You are not used to contempt or pity. If that be so, our marriage will not last.'

" 'Then,' said Sir Gawain (did I ever tell you he was impetuous?), 'be beautiful by day and ugly by night.' Again the lady shook her head.

" 'You will turn from me in the marriage bed. If that be so, our marriage will not last.'

"Then roared Sir Gawain, impetuous Sir Gawain: 'WOMAN! BE WHAT YOU WOULD BE WHEN YOU CHOOSE TO BE THAT!'

"The lady cried out, then, in joy and gladness. 'You have broken the spell! You have broken the spell entire! For that is what a woman wants: *her sovereignty! To be what she would be when she chooses to be that!*'

"And so they spent the night in wedded bliss. In the morning Sir Gawain led his bride out of the bridal chamber, along the long gallery, and down the long stairs to meet all the court. . . ."

"Did she choose to be beautiful?" asked Rosy.

"Did she choose to be ugly?" asked Daisy.

"Whether she was ugly, or whether she was beautiful, is not for me to tell," said Sylvania. "It is *her* story now." There was a silence, as she stared into the coals. Then, in almost a whisper, Sylvania said again: "It is *her* story now."

They sat watching the fire, each thinking her own thoughts. After a while Bear roused himself and came over to Sylvania. He put his great head in her lap. She scratched him gently between the ears, taking care not to touch an old wound.

Came the thaw. Sun warmed, snow melted, roots stirred. One
morning the bear went to the door and tapped with his paw
to show that he wanted to go out. Rosy opened the oaken
door for him, but as his great bulk brushed the frame, his fur
coat caught on the iron haft and tore a rent in his coat. Daisy
whipped out needle and thread to mend it. Too late! He was
gone. Gone for good.

Yet, just for a moment, *just for a moment*, she thought
she may have seen a gleam of gold shine through.

CHAPTER 7

GOING TO TOWN

SPRING CAME AND summer came. All during that time Daisy gathered nettles. Despite the advice in the commonplace book, she stung herself often, but she would not give up. She strewed nettle stalks on the roof of the goat shed to dry, then took them down to the brook, where she pounded them on flat rocks and washed them until the outer sheaths fell off. What she got for all her work, beside stings, was long strands of fiber. Over Rosy's protests, she hung the strands to dry from the rafters in the loft. Finally she spun the fiber into thread. The thread was stronger and silkier by far than the goat hair and wool she usually worked with. It was even finer than the flax threads in the pieces of linen her mother had allowed her to embroider.

At Lammastide, when the grain was ripe, Sylvania decided not to go into the Forest. Instead, the three of them would go across the heath and down into the valley to sell wares at the market in the nearest town. Sylvania had not been to town for years. She had not wanted to go to that place to which her husband went to drink and gamble, where he engaged in trades that shamed her. She dreaded the pity of the women she had grown up with. But now, Sylvania told herself, she was a respected forest gleaner, shopkeeper, and healer. She had not only delicacies and medicines to offer, but knowledge, too. Besides, her girls were growing up. She did not want to keep them in the Forest forever!

Daisy wanted to take the woolen thread she had spun to sell to the weavers. She also packed pieces of embroidered linen to sell in the market. The thread from nettles she would leave at home. She had secret plans for it. Rosy wanted to try her luck with the birch bark boxes she had taught herself to make. Some of them were painted with flowers and birds and little creatures of the Forest.

❧

Daisy and Rosy had never gone so far down the mountain. They marveled at the wide expanse of heath. It seemed to stretch forever. There were almost no trees, only gorse and bracken, grazing sheep and wild ponies. Sylvania allowed them to pause and watch a mare with twin foals, but she hurried them past a tall lonely stone. She said it had been brought there by giants long ago. She pointed out to them the crumbly mawn pools, from which peat had been dug, and showed them a place among the rocks that was still blackened by the fires of ancient miners. Just as they were coming around a crag, they heard the hoarse cries of carrion crows.

Looking upward, they saw a flock of great black birds circling in the sky; one of them was dropping down to settle on something it had seen from the air.

As they rounded the crag, Sylvania and her daughters heard a squeaking cry for help. They came upon a strange sight: a screeching gnome was struggling to elude the clutches of a giant crow. The gnome was no larger than a hare, but he was dressed like a dandy. He wore a coat and trousers of claret-colored velvet and a topaz-colored waistcoat, silk, embroidered with flowers. The bird had its claws embedded in the gnome's jacket and was trying to lift him up and away. Small as the little man had become, Daisy and Rosy still recognized their old acquaintance. The gnome shrieked and cursed at them. When he saw Sylvania, he fell to sobbing and blubbering, whining for help.

Sylvania grabbed him by one arm; Rosy and Daisy each grabbed on to a kicking foot. Thus, for a few moments, they kept the crow from rising. Came the sound of tearing cloth, then the bird flapped off to seek easier prey elsewhere, while both the gnome and his rescuers were dumped unceremoniously onto the heath. The gnome leaped up, shook his fist at the crow, then turned and shook his fist at the three who had sought to save him.

"Now look what you've gone and done," he said. "First you ruin my beard, now you've ruined my velvet coat. I was all dressed up and going to the fair. Now I won't be able to show myself in public. And it's all your fault." The gnome was so ridiculous in his rage, and in his tattered finery, that they could not keep from laughing at him. The Forest Family walked off and left him, still waving his tiny fist. "I'll get you for this," he shouted.

The day at the fair was a great success. They sold their wares so early that they had ample time to wander about the town. Sylvania showed Daisy and Rosy the church and the school she had attended when she was a girl. To her delight, she met old friends who were glad to see her. Hard times had come to some of them. They and their men (if they had not been widowed) were working in the mills. So were their children. Only at August Lammastide and on Christmas Day was the factory closed for holiday. There were rumors that next year not even those days would be counted sacred.

Sylvania's old friends were amazed by the health and high spirits of Daisy and Rosy. When they introduced Daisy and Rosy to their own children, there were a few moments of awkward shyness, but soon Rosy found herself playing hide-and-seek and hopscotch, take-a-giant-step and Simon-sez with the children of the town, just as though she had always done such a thing. When all the children joined hands in a ring to play farmer-in-the-dell and in-and-out-the-windows, she had only to watch for a few minutes before she caught on to the songs and the patterns of the games. Later she explained to her sister, "For this kind of fun, you have to pay attention to yourself paying attention to lots of people, so as to be ready at the right moment."

Daisy was surprised to find herself chattering easily with girls of her own age. She listened to their giggling and whispering about weddings and christenings, about work and wages, about boys and courting, and new ways to braid one's hair. She was glad she had grown up in a house rich with stories. Even if she did not know the actual people who were being talked about, she felt she had already met some of them. The plots and patterns that underlaid the life of the town were surprisingly familiar to her.

"I like talking to those other girls," Daisy said to her mother, half apologizing.

Sylvania was quick to reassure her. "And I like talking to other women. I don't want to live in the town," she said. "I like our life in the Forest. But I have been yearning for your father so much that I forgot the good there is in other women's companionship."

As they wandered among the stalls, each girl, with the money she had earned, was able to buy something that would help her make more money in the future. Daisy had been praised for the strength and evenness of her thread; it had sold quickly. With part of the profits she bought a piece of linen, a silver thimble, and some silken thread for embroidery. She was saving the rest of her money for the day when she could buy a loom. Her secret wish was to weave her nettle thread into the softest cloth imaginable, cloth from which she would make shirts fine enough for princes.

Rosy bought a sharp knife and a small chisel. Her secret plan was to learn how to carve fruits and flowers and little creatures peeking out from under curling leaves. She wanted to make a box like Bernardo had made for her mother, when he was courting her. Just for a moment she allowed herself a pang of regret. She wished that Bernardo had not had to go to war, that he had not been poisoned in his heart, that he could teach her how to use her new tools. "I'll do the best I can without him," she told herself.

After the girls had finished shopping, their mother treated them to gingerbread, and they sat with the other children of the town to watch a play performed on the church steps. People laughed and shouted at the action.

There was Sir George, the farmer-knight, with a saucepan on his head, and a man named John Barleycorn, all covered with straw. They fought with stick swords. When the straw man fell down, the audience cried:

Oh woe, oh woe, look what you've done!
You've murdered our beloved one!
You've struck him down like the noonday sun.

Sir George rushed to the edge of the steps and asked, "Is there a doctor in the house?" The doctor came riding in on a horse that was obviously two people and a broom hiding under an old bedsheet. Everybody roared encouragement. The doctor had a sunburst device on his chest. He stepped forward and cried:

Here comes me, the famous Doctor Gow-win
The bestest doctor in all the tow-win.

Then the doctor and a fat lady, with frizzy hair and a red dress cut low to *there*, poured spirits from a bottle down the straw man's throat (to "enspirit" him) and the devil rushed in, but the lady chased him out. Then the doctor and the lady kissed each other (noisily) and John Barleycorn sprang up, completely restored to life, and an old man, with stars and moons on his costume, said that now the crops would grow again, and everyone shouted and cheered and clapped, and the lady rushed around kissing everybody and collecting money in a frying pan that she said was the Holy Grail.

Sylvania stood up, gathering her baskets and bundles, smoothing her skirt. It was time to go home. Rosie and Daisy said good-bye to their new friends. As they made their way down the street, they heard the town children cry, "Come back! Come back soon."

CHAPTER 8

A LIGHT IN THE SKY

 THE SUN WAS setting as they went back across the heath. "What's that strange light in the sky?" asked Rosy.

"I've never seen such brilliance," said Sylvania.

"It's beautiful!" exclaimed Daisy.

"It's sort of scary," said Rosy, hanging back a little.

Just then they came around a crag and found themselves at that place where they had seen the crows and had rescued the gnome. And there he was again, dandified as ever, even in his tatters. He must have been making himself busy, for he had spread out his precious hoard far and wide across the heath. It was the gleam of his jewels that made such an uncanny glow.

When the gnome saw the Forest Wife and her daughters, he jumped up and down with fiendish glee. "It's mine, all mine!" he said. "I can buy anything I want with it. And what I want is two young girls, plump and pretty. And I'll get them in the end, just see if I don't!"

"Oh, no, you won't!" said Sylvania, putting the girls behind her, so that she stood between them and any danger. "You forget you have me to contend with. I can't be bought and neither can they."

"That's where you're wrong," said the gnome. "I've been waiting for you all day, scattering my jewels so as to lure you back to me. Nowadays I am treated as a gentleman. I will tell people that you surprised me on the heath and that you are three shameless Amazons who tried to rob me of my fortune. I hold the mayor and the judge in the palm of my hand."

Just then there was a deep growl. They all turned to see that a great shaggy bear had come from behind the crag while the gnome was talking. The gnome paled visibly and ran toward Sylvania. "Save me! Save me!" he gabbled. Then, craftily, he said to the bear, "Oh, Beast, don't eat me. See! I'm just a scrap of gristle that'll stick in your craw. Consider first these two young females, so tender and so plump. Or take their mother; she's strong but she's not the least bit tough."

The bear did not let him finish. With one great blow of his paw, he crushed that gnome into grit and sand. Then he stood up on his hind legs and ground every last grain into the soil of the heath. But heed! When the bear stood upright, a

golden gleam shone all 'round about him. His coat split wide; his shaggy fur fell away from him to reveal he was a man.

"Who are you?" asked Daisy, almost blinded.

"I am your father," said the man. "I am Bernardo."

"Where have you been hiding?" asked Rosy.

"I haven't been hiding *all* the time," said Bernardo. He turned toward Sylvania and said, "I was the bear. I was the gnome. Even the Green Knight was part me."

"A little bit of each of them is in you still," she said, "including Sir Gawain." She took his right hand in her two hands and pressed it to her lips. "I have missed you," she said. She looked up into his face and he noticed that a tear ran down from the corner of one eye. He brushed it away from her cheek, gently, with the back of his hand.

"Are you coming home to live with us?" asked Daisy.

"Will you truly be our father again?" asked Rosy.

"If you will have me," he said. "But I must warn you. Life won't be all sunshine. We are not out of the woods yet," said Bernardo. This new Bernardo.

"In the meanwhile," said Sylvania, "we shall live as well as we can among the trees."

"Do you mean that's good enough?" asked Rosy.

"*Dappled* light has its own kind of beauty," Daisy said, unexpectedly.

EPILOGUE

As for those scattered jewels? The rest of them still lie there, cast upon the heath, waiting for another storyteller to come along.

The Forest Family is about the wheel of the cosmos, the wheel of the seasons, and the wheel of life. There are wheels within wheels here, stories within stories.

The Forest Family is a story made out of several others, which you may recognize: "Snow White and Rose Red," from the Brothers Grimm collection, constitutes the main framework on which everything else is hung. "Bearskin," also from Grimm, gives a glimpse of the reality of a soldier's return from the wars. "The Tiger's Whisker," a Vietnamese folktale, was brought back by returning soldiers in the 1960s. I, as teller, have allowed Oriental tiger to become European bear, Oriental wise man to become Green Knight. The soldier's wife is universal.

"Yoke Girl" is adapted from several garbled northern European versions of the "Great Pan Is Dead" myth, including an English folktale, "The King of the Cats." The myth proclaims the precession of the equinoxes, i.e., the ending of an astronomical era, the beginning of a new one. For deeper understanding, see *Hamlet's Mill, An Essay on Myth and the*

Frame of Time, by Georgio de Santiallana and Hertha von Dechend. See also the Greek myths: the battle of Kronos (Time) and Zeus; Phaeton driving his father's chariot (the Sun) recklessly across the sky, thus breaking the axle (the Frame of Time).

The information about making thread from nettles comes from a book by Elizabeth Wayland Barber: *Women's Work: The First 20,000 Years: Women, Cloth, and Society in Early Times*.

Sylvania, the mother in *The Forest Family*, tells "Ruth and Naomi," a story from the Old Testament, as though it had happened in late eighteenth-century Yorkshire. Elements of the Persephone-Demeter story (the round of seasons) creep into the telling.

"The Marriage of Sir Gawain" is a medieval version of an ancient nature myth, which also parallels Persephone-Demeter. Gawain is the Sun God and Lady Ragnall is the Winter Hag. When they kiss at the solstice, the year turns. The Gawain story is well known in ballad form as "The Ballad of Lady Ragnall." It concerns not only the round of the seasons, but the cycle of life: birth, age, death, and rebirth.

"Sir Gawain and the Green Knight" is an elegant thirteenth-century literary poem. I have borrowed some of its images for this retelling of the Marriage story.

The Mummers' Play, performed on the church steps, is a slapstick rendition of the Sir Gawain story, derived from the same body of Celtic lore. Such folk versions are still kept alive in households and villages all over Britain. An

American version, transported across the Atlantic in the eighteenth or early nineteenth century, was discovered by Richard Chase when he was collecting folktales in Virginia and North Carolina in the 1930s. You can find it in his book, *Grandfather Tales*.

Among many guises, the Green Knight is the Green Man, the Wild Man, Bearskin, Iron John. He is Pan and he is Puck. He is John Barleycorn, the corn crop beheaded, *and* he is Saint George, the Great Beheader. He is neolithic farmer and palaeolithic hunter. He is the green and gold maize god of the Iroquois.

As wild nature personified, the Green Knight is the Celtic god Ludd, the life force of ancient Britain. The people who honored him were the Brigantes. They lived near what is now the city of Huddersfield (The Field of Llud). Brighouse means "the seat of the Brigantes." Their chieftain was known by one of his titles, Uther Pendragon, i.e., "the High Dragon of Llud." An Uther Pendragon is purported to be the father of King Arthur.

Bethlehem, the town from whence came Naomi and her husband Elimelach, means "house of bread." I like to think that Sylvania's great-aunts (or their preacher father) had some vague knowledge of Hebrew, which led to confusion of the two towns, Breadhouse and Brighouse.

The Green Chapel is a real place in the Peak District National Park. It is marked (in small faint letters) on British Ordnance Map #118 as *Ludd's Cave*. You can go there! It lies in a hollow hill in Wildboarclough, near Macclesfield. From

Macclesfield, take road A523 south to road A54, turn left (west), toward Allgreave. Cross the bridge over Clough Brook, turn sharp right at the pub, go past Burntcliffe Farm to Grabach Mill. Proceed on foot along the bank of the Dane River, cross the footbridge over Black Brook, take the path that winds upward and to the right. Turn sharp left at the big rock and . . .

GIVE HIM MY LOVE. TELL HIM I SENT YOU.

$ 4 - cen 9/16 k